SCAVENGER HUNT

JANET LORIMER

PAGETURNERS®

www.sdlback.com

ISBN-13: 978-1-68021-401-7
ISBN-10: 1-68021-401-2
eBook: 978-1-63078-802-5

Printed in Malaysia

21 20 19 18 17   1 2 3 4 5

PAGETURNERS® | SPY

Chapter 1

The pot of water on the stove had just started to boil. Erin Holmes was about to add the pasta when the doorbell rang. "Jay," she called. "Can you get that?"

There was no answer. Erin knew her brother was in a bad mood. Having dinner with someone was the last thing he wanted to do. He'd have to sit there and pretend to be nice.

"It'll be boring," Jay had said.

"You'll like Victor. He knows a lot about computers."

"So do I. I'd know more if you would buy me the equipment I need."

"We can talk about it later," Erin had said.

The doorbell rang again.

"Jay!" Erin shouted. "Please get the door. I can't leave the stove."

It was a few seconds later. Erin heard the door open and then close. She could hear Victor talking to Jay. Then she heard the door to Jay's room slam.

Now Victor had come into the kitchen. He was holding a bag.

Erin smiled. "I'm sorry about my brother. He has an attitude tonight."

"It's okay. I get it," Victor said. "I was fifteen once." Then he set the bag on the counter. "I think this will cheer him up. Can you call him in?"

"Jay!" Erin shouted. She turned off the stove. Then she carried the pot to the sink. She was draining the pasta when Jay came into the kitchen.

"What?" he asked.

"Be nice to our guest, Jay," she said.

"I got you something," Victor said. He motioned with his head toward the bag.

Erin looked over at her brother. She hoped he wouldn't embarrass her. But with Jay she never knew. He was an angry kid. And not just tonight. It was normal for him.

Jay was only ten when their parents died. They were killed in a car accident. Erin was twelve years older than him. She'd been given custody of him. She was happy about it. They were able to be together. But raising her brother hadn't been easy. Erin had other responsibilities. She had a full-time teaching job. And she was a part-time student. It was a lot to handle.

Victor had taken a seat on the couch. He was looking at Jay. "I hear you're good with computers."

Jay shrugged.

Erin put the baking dish into the oven. Then she walked over to the couch and sat next to Victor.

"Bring the bag over," Victor said to him. "I think you're going to like what's inside."

Jay grabbed the bag off the counter. He brought it over to the coffee table and set it down. Then he fell back into a chair.

"Go ahead," Erin said. "See what it is."

Jay picked up the bag and looked inside. The look on his face changed in an instant. It went from disgust to stunned surprise. "No way," he said.

"What is it?" Erin asked.

"*Point of Impact*," Jay said.

Erin noticed the way Jay was looking at Victor. It was as if the man had given him a whole store of computer equipment. "Point of what?" Erin asked.

Victor smiled. "*Point of Impact*. It's the hottest new computer game."

"But I know how much a game like that costs." She looked at Victor. "How"— Erin stopped—"You didn't—"

"Yep," Victor said, cutting her off. "I found it in a dumpster. That and a TV. Both were in perfect condition. I figured someone tossed them out by mistake. But you never know. People throw good things out all the time."

"Who would throw out a game like this? Wait. Did you say a dumpster?" Jay asked.

"You mean your sister hasn't told you?" Victor said.

Jay looked at Erin. "What's he talking about?"

"Victor's hobby," Erin said. "And I've tried to tell you about it. But you don't listen. It's that way whenever I mention my friends or coworkers. You don't want to know anything about them. They're old and boring to you."

Jay hadn't heard the last part of what Erin was saying. Or he was ignoring her. "Your hobby sounds cool," Jay said to Victor.

"It's a lot of fun," he said. "I go through trash, looking for treasure."

Erin thought about stopping Victor. She wasn't sure she wanted her brother to hear about this. It might give him ideas.

"I've got some great stories," Victor said. He took off his jacket. Then he draped it over the arm of the couch.

Erin noticed Jay looking at the jacket. It was made of leather. She knew he would love to have one like it. Victor must have also noticed Jay looking at the jacket. "I found that in a dumpster too," he said.

"Really? A leather jacket?"

"Yes," Victor said.

Chapter 2

Erin went into the kitchen. She could hear Victor talking.

"I ran down a dark alley. I didn't know it was a dead end. So I quickly turned around. A security guard was standing there. The guy was built like a professional wrestler. He started to come toward me. I had nowhere to go."

Erin came out from the kitchen. She placed the dish of pasta on the table. Then she called Jay and Victor over. Victor helped himself. Then Erin dished a serving for Jay and herself. But Jay didn't even look at the food.

"So what did you do?" Jay asked Victor.

"It's an old trick. I've used it dozens of times," Victor said. "I pretended someone else was there, and I called out to them. The guard looked away. And I took off running. He tried to grab me as I passed him. But it was too late. I'd gotten away."

Victor told a few more stories during dinner. Jay listened intently. He laughed every now and then. Finally Erin stood up. She began to stack the dishes. Victor smiled. "Dinner was great, Erin. Is there anything I can do to help?"

"Yes. Stop with the stories," she said.

"I can't tell if you're being serious right now," Victor said. "You're just kidding, right?"

"Not entirely," Erin said.

"I like Victor's stories," Jay said. "What's wrong with them?"

"If Victor wants to crawl around in dumpsters, that's his choice. But it's not something that just anyone should do. It can be dangerous." Erin turned to look at Victor. She gave him an angry look. *So shut up*, she was thinking.

"Your sister is right, Jay," Victor said. "I can tell you stories that aren't so funny. They would scare you to death. Dumpster diving isn't for kids."

"I'm not a kid," Jay said. He was looking at Erin when he said it. Then he looked back at Victor. "Tell me what you've found."

"I give up," Erin said. She sat back down.

Victor named some of the things he'd found. Furniture. Clothes. Jewelry. Electronics.

"What made you first think of doing it?" Jay asked.

"It was my first year of college. I had to pay for it myself," Victor said. "It was hard to make enough money from part-time jobs. So I had to find ways to cut costs. One day I was about to throw something into a trash can. I saw a package of pens. They were brand new. Yet someone threw them out.

"That's when I started paying more attention to the trash. I was amazed at what people threw away. Unopened packages and cans just tossed into the garbage. We live in a very wasteful society."

"I think it's criminal to waste so much," Erin said. "So many people are poor or hungry. They would love to have the things people throw away."

"I agree," Victor said. "It's like the old saying. One person's trash is another person's treasure. I know that I've found what I consider to be a few treasures."

"That's why dumpster diving is a good thing," Jay said. "It keeps stuff from going to waste."

"Maybe," Erin said. "But I still think it's dangerous." She picked up the stack of plates. Then she went into the kitchen.

Victor picked up the glasses and followed her. "It *can* be very dangerous," he said to

Jay over his shoulder. "You have to know what you're doing."

Erin started to rinse the plates. That's when she noticed the food that hadn't been eaten. She was about to wash it down the drain. It was the first time she'd really thought about it.

Now Jay was in the kitchen too.

"There are laws about going through people's trash," Victor said. "You can go online and read about it. Basically, garbage that's in a public area is fair game. But taking trash from private property is trespassing. You could be given a ticket or even arrested."

"I want to know where you found the *Point of Impact* game," Jay said.

Erin knew Jay was going to ignore her warning. He'd only heard what he wanted to hear.

Chapter 3

It was five o'clock when Erin woke up the next morning. She should have been asleep. It was Saturday. Instead she lay there, staring up at the ceiling.

She turned over and tried to go back to sleep. But it was no use. After a few minutes, she got up. On her way down the hall, she stopped outside Jay's bedroom. The door was partly open. She thought that was odd. He always slept with the door closed.

Erin tapped lightly on the door. Then she pushed it all the way open. "Jay?" There was no answer. Then she saw that his bed was empty. Maybe he was in the bathroom or in the kitchen. She quickly searched the apartment. But her brother was gone.

It wasn't like him to go out this early. Especially on a Saturday. He slept as late as he could on the weekends. Had he even left a note? Erin looked but didn't find one. Suddenly she was worried. Although it was way too soon to panic.

Maybe it was because of the conversation the night before. The discussion about dumpster diving had left her feeling uneasy. It was all Jay wanted to talk about. He had pumped Victor for information. The best times to do it. Where to find the best stuff. What kind of clothes to wear. What to look out for.

After Victor left, Erin asked Jay to help with the dishes. He even offered to wash them. A little later, she saw him on his cell phone. She knew it was one of his friends. But she hadn't listened to what he was saying. Now she was thinking he'd made plans to go diving.

This is Victor's fault, she thought. Just then she heard the garbage truck outside. Victor had told Jay the best times to search through garbage. It was long before the trucks made their rounds. If Jay had listened, he would have been home by now. Erin had to do something. And Victor would have to help her.

Erin picked up her phone. She speed-dialed Victor. It took him a few rings to answer. His voice sounded like he'd just woken up.

"Jay is gone," Erin said. "I think he's gone dumpster diving."

"What makes you think that?" he asked.

"Are you kidding me? After the way you built it up? He couldn't wait to try it. Besides, where else would he be this early on a Saturday?"

"A friend's house?"

"He would have told me first. Or he would have texted," Erin said.

"Okay," Victor said. "I'll go look for him. Do you want to come with me?"

"Yes. Hurry," Erin said.

Chapter 4

Erin was surprised to hear the knock on the door. It seemed she'd just hung up with Victor. But when she opened it, there he was. He must have sped to the apartment.

Victor stepped past her into the room. "You still haven't heard from him?" Victor asked.

"No," Erin said. "I just called two of his friends. They haven't seen him. Then I called Jay's best friend. He didn't pick up. It's possible the two of them are together. I'm thinking they might have gone searching through trash. After last night, Jay seemed obsessed with the idea."

"You're not blaming me for this, are you?" Victor asked. "Besides, they could be anywhere. You know how kids are. Especially boys. I remember times when I—"

Erin held up her hand. She was signaling for Victor to stop speaking. "I don't want to know," she said. "Let's try and figure out where Jay might be. I know he wanted to find more computer games. Didn't you tell him the best places to look?"

"Yeah. But finding games in those same spots is practically impossible," Victor said.

"Jay doesn't know that," Erin said. "You made it sound so easy. Like there's treasure waiting in every pile of trash."

"Okay, maybe I overdid it. But now we're wasting time." Victor opened the front door and stepped outside. "Let's go find Jay," he said.

Erin followed him out. She locked the door. "Where do we start?"

"I'm thinking of a few places. There's the student housing near the college. Kids throw out all kinds of things. And there are a couple of companies that deal in games. One recycles them. And one sells games and takes trade-ins. It's rare that they throw games out. But it does happen.

"There's also a small company that makes gaming software. I have a friend who works there. He's told me that their security is not always tight. Once a test version of a game was thrown out. Jay would know about this place. I think I even mentioned it to him. We should start there."

They got into Victor's car. Then he pulled out onto the street.

"He should have been home by now," Erin said. "I just hope he's not hurt or worse."

"But you said you think he's with a friend. Wouldn't his friend call for help?"

"If it's Chris, I'm not sure," Erin said. "He doesn't seem like the most responsible kid. But Jay says I don't trust any of his friends."

"You're protective," Victor said. "You have to be. You're both mother and father.

But Jay's too young to understand that." The car slowed. "We're here." He pointed. "This is the company that develops games."

Erin looked out the window. She saw a sign on the building. Aimpoint Games. Under the name were the letters *FTW*. "What do the letters stand for?" Erin asked.

"For the win," Victor said. "It's a common gaming term." He drove to the end of the block. Then he turned into an alley. It backed up against several businesses. One of them was Aimpoint Games. It was at the very end. "Keep an eye out for Jay," he said. "Although he's probably not here. But I need to warn you. The dumpsters are usually inside the fence. If Jay climbed over it, he broke the law."

"What are you saying? That Jay might have been caught?" Erin asked.

"We should check with the police if we don't find him. I don't want to scare you. But if guards caught Jay, they could have gotten rough with him."

Chapter 5

Victor drove slowly toward the end of the alley. Ahead were two police cars. Their lights were flashing.

"It looks like the cops are at Aimpoint," Victor said. He pulled to the side and parked. "I'll be right back."

Erin watched as he walked over to a guard. She noticed that a small crowd of people was beginning to gather. Then she pulled out her phone and called Jay. It went straight to voice mail. "Jay, this is Erin. I'm worried about you. Call me as soon as you get this message."

It was a minute later. Victor came back to the car and got in. "The guard says that a couple of kids were trespassing. It was in the middle of the night. Someone saw them in the dumpster. And they left with something. That's why the cops were called."

"Was it Jay and Chris?"

"I'm not sure. But let's keep searching. I want to check over by the college. That's where I found the game I gave Jay." Victor pulled out of the alley and turned onto the street.

"Do students really throw out things that are still good?" Erin asked.

"It's usually at the end of a semester," Victor said. "They pack as much as they can into their cars. And the rest gets left behind."

◆•◆

After a few minutes of driving around, there was no sign of Jay. "I'm getting scared," Erin said.

"Let's go back to your place," Victor said. "Maybe Jay is there by now."

"But he's not answering his phone. And we haven't searched all the places you mentioned."

"I doubt we'll find him out walking around now. He's probably in his bed asleep," Victor said. He was heading in the direction of Erin's apartment.

"I hope you're right," Erin said. "Are you hungry?" she asked, changing the subject.

"I'm starving," Victor said.

"I'll make us something to eat when we get home."

Victor turned into the parking lot of Erin's apartment and parked his car. As they walked to Erin's door, she looked at Victor. "Jay has to be here," she said. She unlocked the door and pushed it open. Erin could see the back of Jay's head. He was sitting on the couch.

"Jay!" Erin called out. "Are you okay?"

He didn't look up from his phone. "I'm fine," he said. "Why?"

Chapter 6

Erin hurried around to the other side of the couch. "I tried to call you," she said. "And I left messages. But you never called back." Erin sat down next to Jay. "If I wasn't so glad to see you, I'd kill you." She leaned over to give him a hug. Then she quickly straightened in her seat. "You stink! Where have you been?"

"Chris and I were digging around in a lot of garbage. I was just going to take a shower."

"Good idea," Erin said. "Then we can talk about what you've been doing."

Jay got up and walked toward the hallway. Erin watched as Victor moved toward Jay and blocked his way. "You really scared your sister," he said. "Me too."

"But you won't believe what we found," Jay said. He had a smile on his face. Then he pushed past Victor and headed down the hall.

"Oh, I can believe it," Victor called out. "But first tell me one thing. Did you go to Aimpoint Games last night? Were you digging through their trash?"

Erin could hear the anger in his voice.

Jay stopped and turned around. "How did you know?"

"The cops could be looking for you and your friend right now," he said. "I warned you not to trespass. What were you thinking?"

"I know. But its games are epic."

"It doesn't matter," Victor said. "What you did was wrong."

The smile had left Jay's face.

"Come back and sit down," Erin said.

Then she gave Victor a look that said *calm down*. She knew they couldn't be too hard on Jay. He would just take off.

Jay walked back to the couch. Victor followed him. They both sat down.

"This is serious, Jay," Victor said in a calm voice. "The security guard said you took something out of the trash bin. You were on private property at the time. That means you broke the law."

Victor looked over at Erin. "I think Jay should turn himself in. He can tell the cops he didn't know he was breaking the law." He looked at Jay again. "Then you'll return whatever you took." Victor paused. "What was it that you took?"

Jay smiled. "It's another game in the *Destruction* series," he said. "The one you gave me is *Point of Impact*. The one I found must be an older game. I've never heard of it. It's called *Precise Strike*."

"This is worse than I thought," Victor said. "You just don't get it."

"But the game was right there. It was on top of the pile. We didn't even have to dig for it," Jay said.

Victor was starting to get mad again. "*Precise Strike* is brand new. It's not even in the stores yet. Someone made a terrible mistake. They threw out a box they thought was junk. That person probably doesn't work there anymore. But none of that matters. That game hasn't been released yet. Do you know what it means to steal copyrighted material? Aimpoint could press charges. That means you and Chris could go to jail. Where's the game now?"

"Chris has it," Jay said. "He wanted to try it. I came home to get cleaned up first. Then I was—"

Just then Jay's phone rang. He looked at the screen. "It's Chris."

"Tell him not to use the game," Victor said.

Jay answered his phone.

Erin looked at Victor. She shrugged her shoulders. Victor was right. This was serious. And Jay didn't have a clue. Now Erin and Victor were listening as Jay spoke to his friend.

"That can't be right," Jay said. "Are you sure you weren't downloading something else?" Jay paused to listen. "Okay. Bring the game over." Jay hung up. Now he looked annoyed.

"What's wrong?" Erin said.

"Chris says there's something wrong with the game. It started out okay. But then it stopped working."

"Why don't you get cleaned up before Chris gets here," Erin said.

Jay left the room. Erin asked Victor if he still wanted something to eat.

"I'm not hungry," Victor said. "How about some coffee."

"Sure." Erin went to the kitchen. Victor was behind her. "Is espresso okay with you?"

"Make mine a double shot," Victor said.

Erin turned the machine on to heat the water. Then she put ground coffee into the filters and placed two cups underneath. Soon a dark brown liquid was streaming into each of them.

Erin and Victor had each taken a sip when there was a knock on the door. Erin set her cup down. She went to the door and opened it. It was Chris. She led him into the kitchen and introduced him to Victor. Chris put the game on the counter. Just then, Jay came in.

"So what happened?" Jay asked Chris.

"The stupid game crashed my computer," Chris said.

Jay grabbed the game. "You probably did something wrong," he said.

"I did everything the same as usual. It wasn't me."

Victor set his coffee cup down. Then he

took the game from Jay. "Let's look at it on Jay's computer. Maybe I can figure out what's going on," Victor said.

They all went into Jay's room. Victor sat down at the computer and inserted the game. Then he went through the steps to download it. Immediately a dialog box came up.

Precise Strike has encountered a problem and needs to close.

Then the screen went dark.

"No!" Jay shouted.

"I told you," Chris said.

Victor just stared at the screen.

"What happened?" Erin asked.

"The game crashed Jay's computer," Victor said.

Chapter 7

Is this what happened to your computer?" Victor asked Chris.

Chris nodded.

"Okay. So the game you guys found has a virus. I can get rid of the virus on your computers. But you both probably lost a lot of data. I hope you back up your files."

Jay and Chris looked at each other. From the looks on their faces, it was clear they didn't.

"How did the game get a virus?" Chris asked.

"What did it look like when you found it? Was it a loose disc?" Victor asked.

"No. It was in a sealed box," Jay said.

"That's what made it so awesome. It was brand-new software."

"I don't like the sound of this," Victor said.

"Why not?" Jay said. "It's how you found my *Point of Impact* game."

"Not exactly," Victor said. "First of all, I found that game in a dumpster near apartments. And I didn't have to trespass to get to the dumpster. But you did. That should have told you something right from the start.

"Aimpoint keeps some of its dumpsters outside the fence. It would have been okay to look inside those. But the ones behind the fence are on private property. That trash is carried away by a private company. City trash collectors don't touch it. There's a good reason for that," Victor said. "It's how the company protects itself. If a game does get tossed out, no one else can get a copy."

"I'm going to get my coffee," Erin said as she left Jay's room.

Victor followed her. He went into the living room and sat on the couch. Jay and Chris soon joined him.

"What's wrong now?" Jay asked.

"Hold on for a minute," Victor said. "I'm thinking." Then he stood up. "I have to call someone." He walked into the kitchen and started to dial a number.

Erin went out to the living room. After a few minutes, Victor came back. "You can ease up on the boys now," Erin said to Victor. "I'm sure they realize that they did something wrong." But it seemed he hadn't heard her.

"The game started normally when I downloaded it," Victor said. "But after a few minutes of playing, the virus took over. That makes me wonder. Was the game designed with the virus in it?"

Erin shook her head. "You're overthinking it," she said. "Besides, why would someone do that? It's malicious."

"Exactly," Victor said. "Malicious and deliberate. That's what bothers me. Aimpoint is ranked as being one of the best game developers. They're known for consistently creating great games. Gamers love them."

"I don't get it," Chris said. "Why would they do something to ruin their reputation?"

"They wouldn't," Victor said. "Think about it. What would happen if infected games reached the market? It would put an end to Aimpoint. Its reputation and the business."

"But you're saying someone inside the company did this," Erin said.

Victor nodded. "I think it's possible," he said.

"I don't understand," Erin said. "Like Chris said. Why would they want to ruin the company?"

"It's more common than you think," Victor said. "That's why the anti-virus software business is worth billions. I remember reading about a couple of cases. One involved a computer programmer. He worked for a financial services company. Then he was fired. Before he left, he planted a virus. It wiped out thousands of the company's servers. Another person worked at a bank. He thought he was being unfairly blamed for problems with the payroll system. He got revenge by infecting it with a virus."

"So an Aimpoint employee who got fired planted the virus," Erin said. "Is that what you think?"

"It could be that. Or it could be someone who's just unhappy with the company," Victor said. "Maybe they didn't get the raise they'd asked for. You never know what might set someone off. The important thing is to find out who created the virus."

"Why is it up to you?" Erin said.

"I just called a friend of mine who's a

lawyer. She said Jay could go to jail for this. And that we need to find some evidence. We need to figure out who's responsible," Victor said.

"What do you mean by *we*?" Erin asked.

Victor was silent as he looked at Erin.

"Oh no," she said, shaking her head. "You can't be suggesting that I help you with this."

Chapter 8

You have to get inside the company," Victor said to Erin.

"What happened to *we*?" Erin asked. "And what do you mean by 'get inside'?"

"Just listen," Victor said. "I would do it. But I know someone who works at Aimpoint."

"Do what?" she asked.

"Pretend to be an employee," Victor said.

"You're crazy," she said. "What we need to do is call the police. We can explain what the boys did. Tell them about the virus. They'll take it from there."

"Don't you see?" he said. "Whoever created the virus would quickly find out the cops were involved. They'd have time to

39

change their plan. Then they'd keep making infected games.

"Besides, Jay and Chris are already in trouble," Victor said. "With my plan, we have a chance to clear them. And save Aimpoint. What if those games are produced and sold? The cops will think the boys planted the virus."

"This is ridiculous," Erin said. "I can't believe I'm still sitting here listening to you."

"But what if Victor's right?" Jay asked. "I don't want to go to jail."

"We're talking about a sophisticated crime," Erin said. "Why would the police suspect kids?"

"All kinds of people do this sort of thing," Victor said. "Sometimes they're out to do serious harm. Or it's someone who does it for fun. It could even be kids who are bored. They have nothing better to do."

"And how will using me as a spy help?" Erin asked.

"I have a plan," Victor said. "But first I have to call someone." Victor stepped into the kitchen. A few minutes later, he came back. "I called a friend of mine. He keeps up with the gaming industry. I didn't tell him what was going on. I just asked about *Precise Strike*. All the insiders have heard about it. It's supposed to be released soon."

"I thought *Point of Impact* was the hot new game," Erin said.

"It was. But now sales are slowing down. You know how it is with technology. People always want the latest thing. What's hot today is outdated tomorrow. *Precise Strike* will sell like crazy."

"So?" Erin said.

Victor stared at her in silence for a few seconds.

"What's going through your head?" she asked. "You're not still thinking about using me as a spy, are you?"

"There's no other choice," Victor said. "We

have to stop infected games from being sold."

"Well, you better think of another plan. I already have a job, remember?"

"But school just ended for the summer. It's perfect timing. You can apply for a temporary job. Aimpoint always hires extra help when there's a new release." He pulled up a job search site on his phone. Then he typed in Aimpoint. "See. Right there," he said. "They're hiring workers now."

"But I don't know that much about computer games," Erin said.

"You don't have to. These jobs are in packaging. Or you might assist the game developers. They'll have you do simple tasks. You'll have time to find out what we need to know. But you have to get inside."

Erin now felt like she didn't have a choice. Somehow she was at the center of a scandal. A scandal that had nothing to do with her. And the nightmare was just beginning.

Chapter 9

Two days had passed since Victor came up with his plan. Now it was Monday morning. Erin was sitting in Aimpoint's human resources office. She glanced at the clock on the wall. It was ten o'clock and time for her interview. Her thoughts were on the great vacation she'd planned. But now those plans had been cancelled.

Suddenly the door swung open. A man entered the room and sat down behind the desk. He picked up Erin's application and began to review it. When he looked up, she tried to look interested. The man smiled. "How do you feel about working nights?"

♦ • ♦

Twenty minutes later, she left the Aimpoint

building. She crossed the street, then stopped to text Victor. "Interview is over. Meet me at the café near Aimpoint."

As Erin headed for the café, a group of people was walking toward her. She thought one of the people looked familiar. It was a tall young man. But Erin couldn't remember where she'd seen him. Then the group passed her. She had the feeling that at least one of them was looking at her.

When Erin got to the café, she sat down at a table. Then she checked her phone. Victor was on his way. He'd be there in ten minutes. She went up to the counter and ordered two smoothies. Then she paid and gave the clerk her name. Victor came through the door while she was waiting for the order.

"I got the job!" she called out to him. "It's an entry-level position. But at least I'm in. I start tonight at six o'clock."

"That's great," Victor said. "You even sound happy about it."

"It must be the inner spy in me. There's something exciting about going undercover. I feel like I'm part of a secret mission."

"I knew you could do it," Victor said.

The clerk called Erin's name. She went up to get the drinks and then came back to the table.

"Now let's talk about your real job at Aimpoint," Victor said. He told Erin that she'd be looking for information on the employees. Anything negative in their employment history. Then he filled her in on how the company operated. He had a plan for every situation.

Employee records were kept on the computer. Erin was to copy any information she found onto a flash drive. What if she couldn't get onto the computer? Files were also kept in a cabinet. There was one for each employee. Erin should look at those records. Then use her cell phone to take pictures of the damaging documents.

♦ ♦ ♦

That evening, Erin arrived at Aimpoint for her shift. Most of the daytime employees were gone. As soon as she clocked in, the supervisor introduced herself as Kelly.

"I need you to enter sales orders," Kelly said. "There are only a few. But it'll be a good task to start with." She walked Erin over to a computer station. "You'll sit here," she said. "The order entry program is up and ready to go. Just enter the information from each order in the correct fields. I'm going to run over to the café and get something to eat. I should be back in about thirty minutes. Then I'll have something else for you to do."

"Sounds good," Erin said.

"I'll give you the system passwords when I get back," Kelly said. Then she left the building.

Erin quickly entered the orders into the system. Then she found the cabinet with the employee files. Luckily it was unlocked. She opened it and saw it was arranged in alphabetical order.

As Erin took out the first file, she had to remind herself. *What I'm doing isn't a crime. It's for a good cause.* That's what Victor had told her.

There were files for about thirty employees. Erin started to think about how long this could take. She had to read the information in each file. Pick out the negative information. Then copy it.

Her supervisor would only be gone for thirty minutes. This could be a slow process. Maybe when she was able to access the computer files, it would go faster. Hopefully she wouldn't get caught. Erin opened the first file and started to read.

Chapter 10

It was Friday evening. Erin had been working at Aimpoint for nearly a week. She had gathered information on several employees. They were possible suspects. She'd copied everything onto one flash drive. She arranged to meet Victor at the café before work. "Mission accomplished. Bring your laptop," she'd texted him.

Victor was already there when she walked into the café. She sat down at his table.

"After this, I don't think we should meet here," Victor said. "Some of your new friends might wonder who I am. It's best if we aren't seen together."

"What new friends?" Erin asked. "I spend all my time spying and trying not to get caught. I don't have time to make friends. And don't forget. I also have to do the job I was hired for."

"No friends?" Victor said. "I saw that group of people who just walked in. Some of them were smiling and waving to you."

Erin glanced over her shoulder. It was the same group she saw at work every night. She hadn't officially met them. But they'd always smiled at each other. It was like before. Erin had a feeling that she knew a couple of them from somewhere else. Was it her teaching job? Or the college classes she was taking?

"Relax," Victor said. "You're acting like you're guilty of something."

"No kidding," Erin said.

"So what did you find out?" he asked.

Erin handed him the flash drive. He inserted it into his laptop. Then he began to click on files. After a few minutes, he looked up at her. "From what I can see, there are three strong suspects. Patrick Allen, Brandon Lee, and Kelsey Price. Which one do you think wanted revenge on Aimpoint? Do you have a feeling about it?"

"I do," Erin said. She looked over her shoulder. Then she turned back to Victor. "Kelsey Price," she said in a low voice.

"What makes you say that?" he asked.

"She's been written up the most. She was caught complaining about her boss on social media. And she's gossiped about him to other employees. In general, she has a bad attitude."

"It sounds like she's capable of revenge," Victor said. "But look at this. Patrick Allen was passed over twice for a promotion. That would make someone angry enough to want revenge."

"Yes," Erin said. "What about Brandon Lee? Can we eliminate him as a suspect?"

Victor shook his head. "I don't think

so. He was recently criticized for doing bad work. And listen to this. He was suspected of passing company secrets to a competitor."

"That's serious. Does it say in the file why they didn't fire him?"

"It says right here," Victor said, reading from the file. "No solid proof. Still, this doesn't make him look good." He closed the files and pulled the flash drive from his laptop. "Have you met any of these people? Do you know where they sit?"

"No. So far I've been stuck in the business office."

Victor shut his laptop. "You know what your next step is, right?"

Erin nodded. "Find out more about the suspects."

The first thing Erin wanted to do was find out where the suspects sat. Maybe she would find some evidence in their cubicles. It was later that evening when Erin got her chance. Kelly finally left the building for her break.

Erin walked around the office. She carried a stack of gaming magazines. They were addressed to the developers. In case anyone asked her, she could say she was distributing them.

Most of the cubicles were now empty. Erin read the name plate as she passed each cubicle. When she reached Patrick Allen's workstation, no one was there. But it seemed to Erin that he was still at work. His desk lamp was on. And one of his desk drawers was open. Maybe he went to the staff kitchen to get a cup of coffee.

She was about to place a magazine on the desk. That's when her hand touched the mouse. The computer had been in sleep mode. Now a document appeared on the screen. Erin knew it was code of some kind. She pulled out her phone. Then she took a picture of the computer screen and forwarded it to Victor.

Just then, Erin felt a hand on her shoulder. She jumped and spun around to face whoever it was. A man was standing there.

"What are you doing?" he asked.

Chapter 11

You scared me," Erin said. "Are you Patrick Allen?" She was thinking that he looked familiar. Like she knew him from somewhere.

"Yes," he said. He wasn't smiling. Then he repeated the question. "What are you doing?"

"I'm delivering these magazines," Erin said. "I set one right there next to your computer." She thought about explaining how she'd accidentally brought his document up. But then she decided not to. It was best to say as little as possible.

Now Patrick was looking at the screen. He opened his mouth like he was going to say something. Then he looked back at Erin. "Thanks," he said.

"I'd better get going," Erin said. She smiled and started to walk away.

"You're new here, aren't you?" Patrick asked.

Erin stopped and turned around.

"Yes. I just started on Monday. I'm still getting used to everything." As she looked at Patrick, her mind was racing. Erin knew she had seen him somewhere. Then she remembered. It was in the café. But there was somewhere else she'd seen him. She turned and started walking.

"What was your name?" Patrick called.

"Erin," she said, looking back over her shoulder. Then she hurried down the aisle. Erin finished delivering the magazines as quickly as she could. Then she went back to the business office. Luckily her boss was not there. Erin looked at her phone. Victor had answered her text about the code.

"It's virus code," he'd texted.

Erin called him. He picked up right away.

"We caught him," Erin said. "I didn't think it would be this easy. Now what? Do we call the police?"

"Hold on," Victor said. "I'm not sure if it's the cops we want or—"

At that moment Erin heard her boss come into the room. "I have to go," Erin whispered. "Figure out what to do next. Then call me back."

Kelly was now looking at her. "Okay. You can stay up for another hour," Erin said into the phone. She was pretending to talk to someone. "And then you go to bed," she said. Erin looked up at her boss and smiled. "Hi. I was just checking on my brother. I hope that's okay."

"Sure," Kelly said.

Erin went back to work. She was entering data into a spreadsheet. An hour later, she got a text from Victor. "Can you meet me outside the café?"

"My break is in thirty minutes."

"I'll be in my car. See you then."

♦ • ♦

At break time, Erin hurried to meet Victor. He was standing outside his car. When Erin reached him, Victor motioned for her to get inside. Then he got into the car.

"Have you figured out a solution?" Erin asked.

"First tell me what happened," Victor said.

Erin told him how she'd found Patrick's cubicle. Then she accidentally saw the virus code. "I'm glad you'd showed me some code," Erin said. "I might not have known what it was."

"How did the guy act when he found you in his cubicle?" Victor asked.

"He might have been a little suspicious. I was probably acting really nervous. That's because I was. He didn't make a big deal about it. But it could have been an act."

"I've been doing a lot of thinking," Victor said. "And I've changed my mind. We should go to the police. We can take Jay with us and show them the computer game he took."

"Do you want to go first thing tomorrow morning?" Erin asked.

"I don't think we should wait that long," Victor said. "Patrick might be suspicious. He could destroy all the proof."

"So we're going tonight? What about work? I'm not off for another four hours."

"Then we'll go when you get off work. Why don't you call Jay? Tell him when to be ready."

Erin's phone rang just then. She looked at the screen and then looked at Victor. "I don't recognize the number," she said.

"Could it be Jay using a friend's phone?" Victor asked. "You better answer."

"Hello," Erin said. There was silence on the other end. "Hello," she repeated.

"You will do exactly what I say. If you don't, you will never see your brother again." Erin couldn't tell if the voice belonged to a man or a woman. She thought it sounded like someone trying to disguise their voice.

"Where's Jay?" Erin cried out.

Then the caller gave her instructions.

Chapter 12

Jay's been kidnapped," Erin told Victor.

Victor's eyes were wide. "Kidnapped? What did the caller say? Was it a man?"

"I couldn't tell if the caller was a man or a woman. But he says he'll return Jay in exchange for the game."

"Wait a minute. You just said you couldn't tell if the kidnapper was a man or a woman."

"Come on, Victor. It has to be Patrick, doesn't it?"

Victor shook his head. "I saw him go inside the café. It was just before you got here. I watched him order. Then he left with a cup of coffee."

"But that doesn't make sense. There's coffee at Aimpoint. He could have gotten it there. Did you see him use his phone?"

Victor shook his head.

"So he wasn't the one who called me," Erin said. She was still holding her phone. "I'll call Jay. Maybe this was some kind of prank."

Erin called her brother, but he didn't answer. "It's going straight to voice mail," she said to Victor. She listened to Jay's recording, then left a message for him to call her back.

"Maybe he went to a friend's house," Victor said.

"Oh, that's right," Erin said. She opened the car door. There was an angry look on her face. "You would know. That's where Jay was the last time he didn't answer my call. He was with Chris. They were dumpster diving."

"There you go again. You're blaming this on me," Victor said.

"Whatever. Right now, Jay's life could be in danger. I'm not going to wait around for him to call me back. I have to do something now." Erin got out of the car.

"You're right," Victor said before she slammed the door. He got out of the car and hurried over to her side. "We'll go to the police right now."

By now Erin was walking toward her car. It was in Aimpoint's lot. She stopped and turned to look at Victor. "No police. That was part of the kidnapper's instructions. And now I do think it's Patrick."

"But how does he know you have the infected game?" Victor asked.

They had reached her car. "Good question," Erin said as she unlocked the door. All of a sudden, an image came into her head. It was Patrick.

"That's it!" she said. "I finally remember

where I first saw him. It was in the alley behind Aimpoint. He was standing with a group of people. They were watching the cops. It was when you stopped to talk to that guard. Do you remember?"

Victor was thinking back. Finally he nodded. "Right. I do remember."

"He probably wrote down your license plate number. Traced the car somehow," Erin said.

"Then, when he saw you working at Aimpoint—"

"We need to go," Erin said. Then she got into the car and started it. "I need to get the game first. Follow me to my place," she said as she closed the door. Then she drove to her apartment. Victor was right behind her. They pulled into the parking lot of her apartment building and parked.

Erin got out of her car. Victor rolled down his window. "I'll grab the game and be right back," she said. "We'll take my car."

A few minutes later, Erin returned to the car. Victor was standing there, ready to go. She handed him the game and two flashlights. They got into her car, and Erin pulled out onto the street.

"Where are we going?" Victor asked.

"The caller said to go to the disposal station," Erin looked over at Victor. He had a confused look on his face. "The city dump," she said. "That's where the exchange is supposed to happen. If it weren't so serious, it would almost be funny. I mean, this whole nightmare started in a dumpster. And now we're going to be surrounded by trash."

After a few miles of driving, Erin came to the turnoff for the dump. She turned onto the road and drove to the entrance. Ahead were several large dumpsters for recyclables. Erin parked, and they got out of the car.

They passed the trash bins and headed for the landfill. Erin covered her nose and mouth. "It smells so bad," she said. Then she heard noises that sounded like scratching. Erin guessed that it was rats rustling around, looking for food. There were probably cockroaches too.

"Exactly where are you supposed to make the exchange?" Victor asked.

"Stop! Don't turn around," a voice said. It had come from behind them.

Erin thought there was something odd about the voice. It was deep. But it sounded forced. Like a woman was trying to sound like a man. This had to be the kidnapper.

"Do you have the game?"

"I have it," Erin said. "Where's my brother?"

"First give me the game," the voice said.

Erin started to turn around. But the voice stopped her in her tracks. "I said don't turn around! Slowly set the game on the ground."

"Don't give it up until we know Jay's okay," Victor said.

"Shut up!" the voice said.

"Okay," Erin said. "I'll give it to you." She reached into the pocket of her jacket and pulled out the game. Then she heard footsteps. Erin quickly turned around. All she could see was the moonlight reflecting off the barrel of a gun. Now she was holding the game behind her back. "Don't come any closer!" she called out into the darkness. "Where is my brother? I want proof that he's all right."

Chapter 13

The little punk is over there in a dumpster," the kidnapper said. "Now give me the game."

"Victor!" Erin shouted. "Go check on Jay!" Even though she was trying to sound tough, Erin was shaking with fear.

"Neither of you move!" the kidnapper shouted. "I'll use the gun if I have to."

But Victor had already moved a few steps toward the dumpster. The kidnapper shifted the gun from Erin to Victor and back to Erin again.

"Stop!" the kidnapper's voice cried out. Victor froze.

Now Erin was certain it was a woman's

voice. But if this wasn't Patrick, who was it? Just then, a groan came from the direction of the dumpster. "Here!" she called out to Victor. "Take the game." Then she tossed it to him.

The kidnapper turned the gun on Victor. That's when Erin ran to the dumpster. Inside she saw her brother. He'd been tied up and gagged. Erin removed the gag from his mouth. "Are you all right?" she asked.

Jay wasn't able to speak, and he was trembling. Erin thought he must be in shock. She helped him climb out of the dumpster and loosened the ropes. Then she took off her jacket and put it around him.

"You got what you want," the kidnapper said. "Now give me the game."

Erin looked over at Victor. He needed to do something quick. Either give the kidnapper the game or somehow get the gun. Why was he stalling?

"Okay," Victor finally said. "Here's the game. Take it." He drew back his arm like he was about to toss the game. But before he could it, the sound of sirens filled the air.

"No!" The kidnapper swung around toward Erin and Jay.

Before the kidnapper could fire the gun, Erin pushed her brother behind the dumpster. Just as she threw herself to the ground, a bullet hit the container above her body.

The sound of the sirens were now getting closer. And soon the lights from the police cars lit up the area. Erin could see the kidnapper. It was a woman after all. She tried to fire the gun, but it jammed. That's when she threw it onto the ground. And then she took off running toward the landfill.

The police cars were now stopped. The

cops had gotten out of their cars. Erin ran over to them. "She went that way," Erin said, pointing toward the trash.

One of the cops ran in that direction. The other cop stayed behind to ask her and Victor questions. Then he called an ambulance for Jay.

Erin walked toward the landfill. She was trying to see what was happening. From out of the darkness, two figures approached. It was the cop and the woman. Erin didn't think. She just started moving toward her. "Who are you?" Erin asked.

The woman didn't say anything.

"You're lucky the cops got here when they did. I was about to go after you myself," Erin said. She watched as the cop walked the woman to one of the cars and helped her inside. Then the ambulance arrived. The medics examined Jay. Erin and Victor were standing nearby.

"That was pretty gutsy of you to threaten the kidnapper," Victor said.

Erin smiled. "I would have buried her in all that trash."

"Remind me not to mess with you," he said.

"How did the police know to come here?" Erin asked.

"I called them when we stopped to pick up the game," Victor said.

The medics were loading Jay into the ambulance. "I'd like to go with him," she said to one of the crew. Then she handed her car keys to Victor. "We'll meet you at the hospital," she said. He nodded, then Erin got into the ambulance.

Later at the hospital, a doctor examined Jay. He was in shock and dehydrated. But he would make a full recovery. The police were there, waiting to interview him. First they spoke with Victor and Erin. Victor explained what had happened. By this time, Jay was asleep. The police said they would come back in the morning.

Victor and Erin left the hospital. They agreed to meet back there early the next morning.

◆ ◆ ◆

When Erin arrived at the hospital, Victor wasn't there yet. But Jay was awake. He was speaking to police when she walked into his room.

"Your brother has been cleared of any wrongdoing," an officer said. "We made an arrest." He explained to Erin what they'd discovered. Then the officers left.

Just as the door closed behind them, it opened again. Victor was standing there. "What did I miss?" he asked.

"The police made an arrest," Erin said.

"We know it was a woman. Kelsey Price, right? Although it was Patrick who had the virus code. I'm confused."

"It was all three of our suspects. Kelsey, Patrick, and Brandon. They all had their own reasons to hurt the company. So they got together and came up with the virus scheme. But then the infected game Jay found got thrown out by accident. The three of them panicked. They had to get it back before someone figured out what they were up to. That's when they decided to kidnap Jay."

Victor walked over to the bed. "Hey, Jay," Victor said. "You've sure had a rough time lately. I bet you don't even want to think about video games."

"Not the ones that people throw away," Jay said. "I've decided to design my own game."

"Oh really," Victor said. "Will it be like *Point of Impact*? You could make a fortune."

"It's kind of like that," Jay said. "I'm calling my game *Salvage Slayers*."

Victor smiled. "*Salvage* as in junk,"

he said. "And it's a game about dumpster diving. I like it. I'll be your first customer."

"Great," Jay said. "Now if I can get my sister to buy me some new hardware."

"I have a surprise for you when you get home," Erin said.

"New hardware?" Jay asked.

Erin smiled. "I'd rather you be obsessed with something that doesn't involve danger." Then she laughed. "Well, at least not physical danger."

"Hey, Victor. When are you going dumpster diving again? I need stories for my game."

"Oh no," Erin said, looking at Victor.

"It's for a good cause," Victor said. "*Salvage Slayers*."

Comprehension Questions

Recall

1. Why did Erin have custody of her younger brother?

2. Where did Erin and Victor meet the kidnapper?

3. Why were Jay and Chris in trouble with the police?

Identifying Characters

1. Which character got a temporary job at Aimpoint?

2. Which character warned Jay about illegal dumpster diving?

3. Which character caught Erin staring at his computer screen?

Drawing Conclusions

1. When Erin learned that Jay had been kidnapped, why didn't she call the police?

2. Why did Jay's computer crash when he tried to load *Point of Impact*?

Vocabulary

1. Erin said that designing a game with a virus in it was malicious. What does *malicious* mean?

2. Victor asks Jay about stealing copyrighted materials. What is a copyright?

3. As Victor told stories of dumpster diving, Jay listened intently. What does *intently* mean?